I FEEL GOOD!

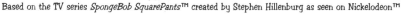

Based on the TV series *SpongeBob SquarePants*™ created by Stephen Hillenburg as seen on Nickelodeon™

SIMON SPOTLIGHT/NICKELODEON

An imprint of Simon & Schuster Children's Publishing Division

New York London Toronto Sydney

1230 Avenue of the Americas, New York, New York 10020

SpongeBob Goes to the Doctor © 2005 Viacom International Inc. *Behold, No Cavities!: A Visit to the Dentist* © 2007 Viacom International Inc. All rights reserved.
NICKELODEON, *SpongeBob SquarePants*, and all related titles, logos, and characters are trademarks of Viacom International Inc. Created by Stephen Hillenburg.
All rights reserved, including the right of reproduction in whole or in part in any form.
SIMON SPOTLIGHT and colophon are registered trademarks of Simon & Schuster, Inc.
For information about special discounts for bulk purchases, please contact Simon & Schuster Special Sales at 1-866-506-1949 or business@simonandschuster.com.
Manufactured in the United States of America 0810 LAK
First Edition 2 4 6 8 10 9 7 5 3 1
ISBN 978-1-4424-0783-1
These titles were previously published individually by Simon Spotlight.

SpongeBob Goes to the Doctor

by Steven Banks
based on the screenplay written by Paul Tibbitt, Ennio Torresan Jr., and Mr. Lawrence
illustrated by Zina Saunders

SpongeBob woke up one morning feeling terrible. "Oh, Gary, I don't feel like myself," said SpongeBob. "AH-CHOO!" When SpongeBob sneezed, pink bubbles blew out of all his holes.

"Meow," said Gary.

"Don't be silly, Gary," said SpongeBob. "I don't have a cold. I don't get colds, I get the suds."

"Meow," Gary replied.

"No! I can't get the suds!" cried SpongeBob. "Then I'd have to miss work, and I can't miss a day of working at the Krusty Krab!"

"SpongeBob, what's holding up those Krabby Patties?" yelled Mr. Krabs.
"Coming right up, sir," said SpongeBob, sniffling.
Mr. Krabs poked his head through the window. "What's wrong with you, boy? You're paler than a baby sea horse! Do you have the suds?"
"No, sir!" said SpongeBob weakly. "I feel great! AH . . . AH . . . AH-CHOO!"

"SpongeBob, you're too sick to work," said Mr. Krabs. "Go home and get some rest."

"No, Mr. Krabs," said SpongeBob, pleading. "I'm okay! Honest!"

"Nothing personal, lad," said Mr. Krabs. "But I can't have you sneezing all over my food!"

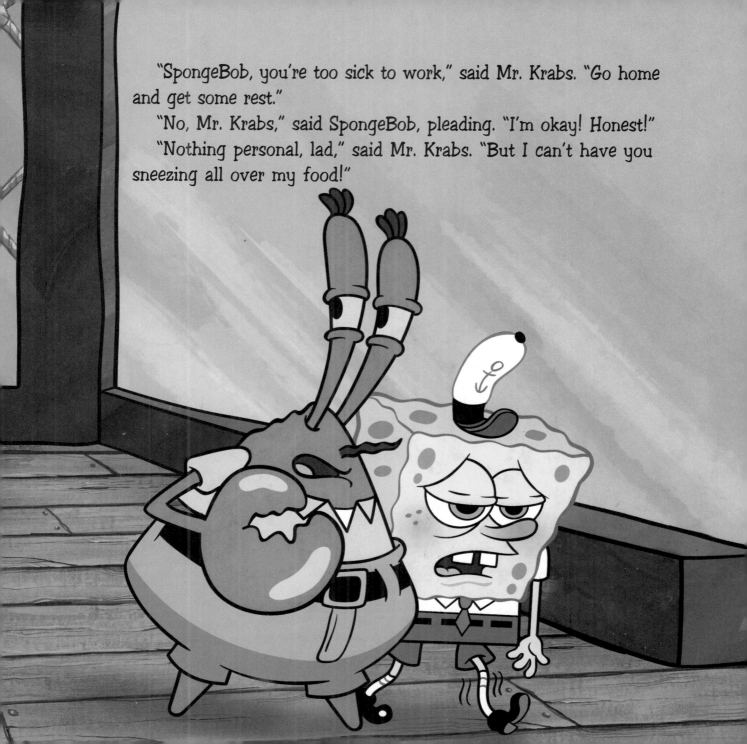

"Who am I kidding, Gary? AH-CHOO! I've got the suds," said SpongeBob sadly. "I'd better go see the doctor before I get worse."

SpongeBob called up his friend Sandy Cheeks. "Sandy, I'm sick. Can you take me to the doctor?"

"Sure, SpongeBob!" said Sandy. "I'll be there faster than you can say 'Sandy, I'm sick. Can you take me to the doctor?'"

"Hey, SpongeBob. Going skiing?" asked Patrick.

"I'm sick, Patrick," said SpongeBob, sniffling. "I'm going to the doctor."

"No!" cried Patrick. "You can't go to the doctor!"

"Why not?" asked SpongeBob.

Patrick pushed SpongeBob back into his house. "I know a guy who knows a guy who went to the doctor's office once. It's a horrible place!"

"The doctor's office can't be as horrible as the . . . AH-CHOO! . . . suds,"
said SpongeBob.
"Yes, it is," said Patrick. "First they make you sit in the . . . *waiting room*!"

"Is that the horrible part?" asked a nervous SpongeBob.

Patrick shook his head. "No! It gets worse! They make you read . . . *old magazines!*"

"Oh, no!" cried SpongeBob. "I'm scared. I don't want to go to the doctor!"

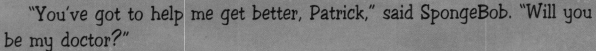

"You've got to help me get better, Patrick," said SpongeBob. "Will you be my doctor?"

Patrick scratched his head. "Well, I didn't go to doctor school, and I don't know anything about medicine, but sure! I'll do it!" Patrick started putting corks into all of SpongeBob's holes. "There. That ought to do the trick!" he said, clapping his hands.

"Do you feel better now, SpongeBob?" asked Patrick.

"I . . . I . . . AH . . . AH . . . AH-CHOO!" SpongeBob sneezed, and he blew up like a balloon. "No bubbles!" said SpongeBob excitedly. "Doctor Patrick, it looks like your treatment is working!"

"I'll send you my bill in the mail," said Patrick.

"I'll be cured in no time," said SpongeBob. "I should call Sandy and tell her she doesn't need to take me to the doctor."

SpongeBob tried to push the buttons on the phone, but his fingers were too big and puffy. "Doctor Patrick, will you call Sandy for me?" he asked.

"Hello, Sandy, this is Doctor Patrick. I'm calling on behalf of my patient, Mr. SquarePants. You don't need to take him to the doctor."

"Patrick, you're not a doctor!" said Sandy. "Tell SpongeBob I'll be there faster than a barefoot jackrabbit in a race!"

"Sandy's coming, and she's bringing a jackrabbit!" cried Patrick.
"You've got to make me well or she'll take me to the doctor!" yelled SpongeBob.

"I know exactly what to do," said Patrick. He put a giant bandage on SpongeBob's nose, spread jellyfish jelly on his feet, and played a song on the accordion. "Do you feel better?" he asked.

"No!" said SpongeBob. "And Sandy's going to be here any second!"

Sandy pounded on SpongeBob's door. "Open up!" she yelled.

"I'm sorry. There's nobody home," called Patrick.

"Where's SpongeBob?" Sandy asked.

"Uh, he's not here at the moment," said Patrick. "Please leave your message after the beep. *Beep!*"

Sandy karate-chopped the door down. "Patrick, I am taking SpongeBob to see a real doctor!" She pushed SpongeBob out the door and rolled him down the road.

"He's fine!" cried Patrick, running after her. "Tell her how fine you are, SpongeBob!"

"I'm . . . AH-CHOO . . . fine!" said SpongeBob.

SpongeBob started rolling down the hill toward the Krusty Krab!
"SpongeBob, stop!" shouted Mr. Krabs. "You can't come back to work!
You're still sick. Plus, there's no way you'll fit into your uniform now!"

SpongeBob rolled up to the front door and sneezed a giant sneeze.

"AH-CHOO!"

There was no denying it. SpongeBob needed a *real* doctor.

He went to see the best doctor in Bikini Bottom.

"Well, Mr. SquarePants, you have the suds," said the doctor. "Are you ready for your treatment?"

"Are you going to make me wait in the waiting room and read old magazines?" asked a worried SpongeBob.

The doctor laughed. "No, silly. I'll give you some medicine, and you'll feel all better!"

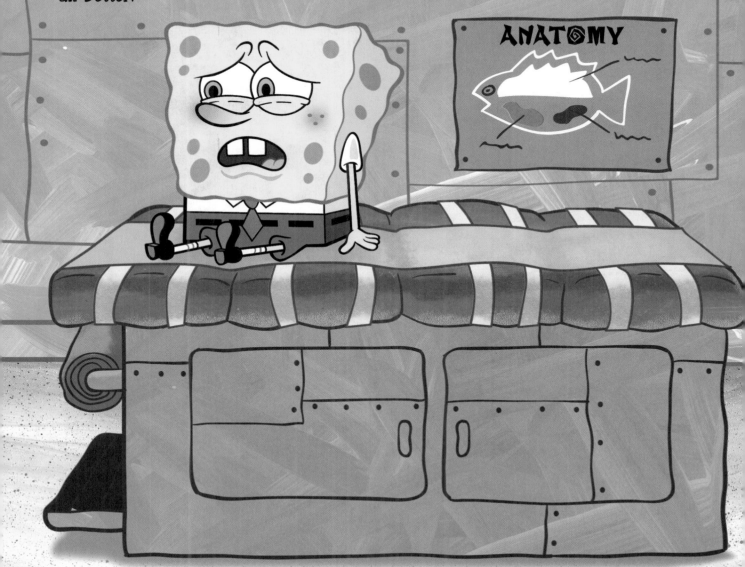

Patrick and Sandy were waiting for SpongeBob in the waiting room.

"SpongeBob, you're all better!" said Sandy. "Aren't you glad you saw the doctor?"

"I sure am!" said SpongeBob. "Hey, Patrick? Are you enjoying that old magazine you're reading?"

Patrick screamed, "Old magazine! NOOOOOOO!" And he ran away as fast as he could!

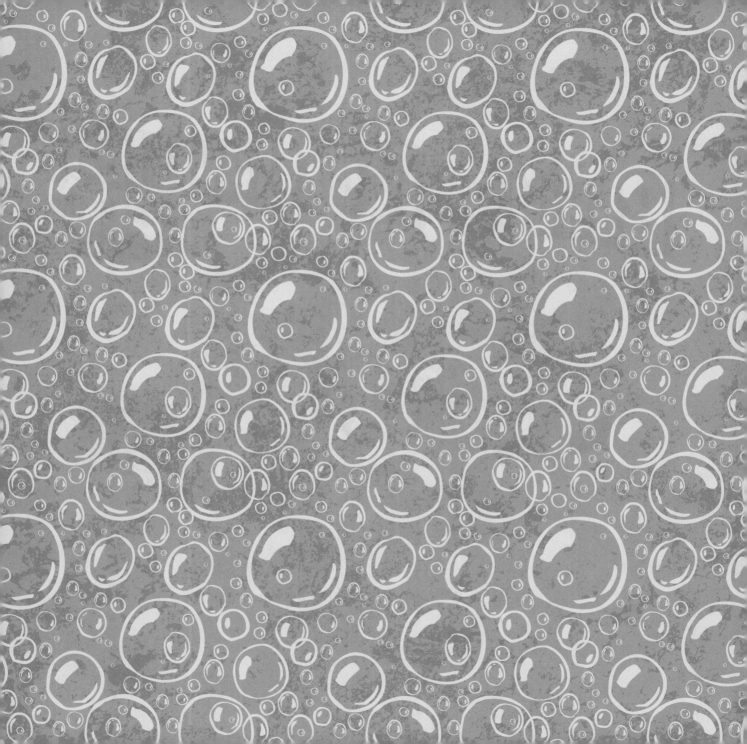

BEHOLD, NO CAVITIES!
A Visit to the Dentist

by Sarah Willson illustrated by Harry Moore

"Today is the day! It's finally here!" said SpongeBob as he bounded out of bed one morning.

"Meow!" said Gary.

"That's right, Gary. It *has* been exactly six months, two hours, and seven minutes since my last dental cleaning. So today I get to go again!"

SpongeBob raced off to brush his teeth extra carefully.

Patrick came to visit while SpongeBob was still brushing.
"SpongeBob! What's wrong? You're foaming at the mouth!" he cried in alarm.

"Ish jusht tooshpashte, shilly," said SpongeBob, spitting out the toothpaste and showing Patrick his dazzling smile. "I flossed and now I'm brushing with my favorite toothbrush, just as I do each morning and night."

"Oh! I always wondered what that thing was," said Patrick, pointing at SpongeBob's toothbrush.

SpongeBob's mouth dropped open. "You don't floss or brush your teeth, Patrick?"

"Nope."

"Or . . . have semiannual dental exams?"

"Nuh-uh."

"Have you *ever* been to a dentist?"

"What's a dentist?"

"Patrick, ol' buddy," he said when he had found his voice. "I think you had better come along with me to see my dentist, Dr. Gill, today. I'll call and make an appointment for you."

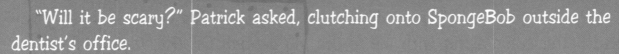

"Will it be scary?" Patrick asked, clutching onto SpongeBob outside the dentist's office.

SpongeBob smiled. "No, Patrick. Dr. Gill's office is the friendliest place in the world. And what's more, I am their favorite patient. Everyone here knows me! Just watch." He threw open the door.

"Hello! And who are you, young man?" asked the receptionist.
"I thought everyone here knew you," whispered Patrick.
"She must be new," SpongeBob whispered back.

"SpongeBob! You're here!" shrieked a voice.

"Hi, Debbie!" called SpongeBob. "Debbie is Dr. Gill's hygienist," he told Patrick. "She's the person who cleans your teeth."

"Do I hear SpongeBob?" called another voice.

"Hi, Dr. Gill!" said SpongeBob. "Dr. Gill makes sure you don't have any cavities, but if you do he'll fix them."

Just then Debbie and Dr. Gill burst into the waiting room. They joined
hands with SpongeBob and sang their favorite song:
   "I brush and floss my teeth each day
   To ward away that tooth decay!"

"Gee," said Patrick. "I had no idea getting your teeth cleaned could be this fun."

"Oh, Patrick," said SpongeBob, "you haven't seen *anything* yet!" He pulled Patrick into a hallway and pointed. "Behold! The No Cavi-Tree!"

"Wow. Why is it full of teeth that say 'SpongeBob'?" asked Patrick.
"Because you get your name posted up there when you have no cavities at your checkup!" SpongeBob replied. "I get a new tooth every time I come because I have never had a cavity."

"Time for your cleaning, SpongeBob!" called Debbie cheerfully. "First let's take a new X-ray."

Next Debbie cleaned SpongeBob's teeth. Then she polished his teeth with the bubble-gum-flavored tooth polish he chose, rinsed his teeth, and suctioned the water out of his mouth with Mr. Thirsty.

SpongeBob giggled. "That Mr. Thirsty always tickles!"

Then Dr. Gill had a look. "Your teeth look very healthy," he said. "We won't know for sure until we see the X-rays, but you certainly are a model dental patient!"

"Thanks, Dr. Gill," said SpongeBob. "Now it's time for you to look at my friend Patrick's teeth. He's never been to the dentist before."

Patrick got in the chair and opened his mouth. Debbie and Dr. Gill took turns peering in. Dr. Gill buzzed the receptionist. "Cancel the rest of the appointments today," he said. "This will take awhile."

Some hours LATER . . .

Finally Patrick's teeth were clean. "You can each go pick out a brand-new toothbrush now," Debbie said.

"Follow me, Patrick! I can't wait to see what colors they have!" cried SpongeBob.

"Oh, boys," called Dr. Gill. "I just learned that the light box we use to view your X-rays needs a new bulb. Why don't you go home and I'll call you both tomorrow with the results of your X-rays? By then the box will be fixed."

The next morning Patrick burst into SpongeBob's house. "No cavities!" he yelled. "Dr. Gill's receptionist called and told me! I get to have my name on the No Cavi-Tree!"

"Patrick! That's great!" said SpongeBob.
BRIIIING!

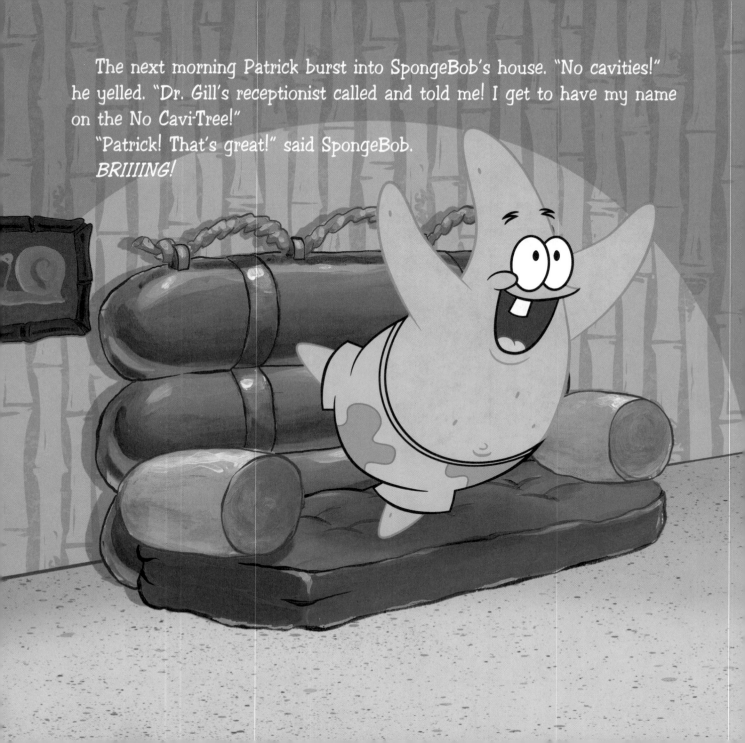

SpongeBob answered his phone. "Yes, this is SpongeBob. I . . . I . . . *what?* Okay. I'll be there at two o'clock. Buh-buh-buh-bye." SpongeBob hung up the phone and burst into tears. "I have four cavities!" he sobbed.

"I'll come with you to get them filled, old buddy," Patrick said, patting his friend on the back.

That afternoon Patrick accompanied his friend to the dentist's office. SpongeBob's eyes welled up with fresh tears as they walked past the No Cavi-Tree.

"Hello again, SpongeBob and Patrick," said Dr. Gill. He looked at SpongeBob's X-rays. "It seems you have . . . wait. These aren't *your* X-rays!"

"They're not?" asked SpongeBob in a small voice.

"No! These are *Patrick's*! My new receptionist must have mixed them up!"

"I have no cavities?" said SpongeBob. "I HAVE NO CAVITIES!" he cried, leaping out of the chair with excitement.

"Woo-hoo! Way to go, SpongeBob!" shouted Patrick joyfully. Everyone linked arms and danced merrily. Suddenly a thought dawned on Patrick and he stopped dancing. "But that means *I* have cavities."

Debbie patted the chair. "Hop up, Patrick," she said kindly. "Dr. Gill will have these filled in a jiffy."

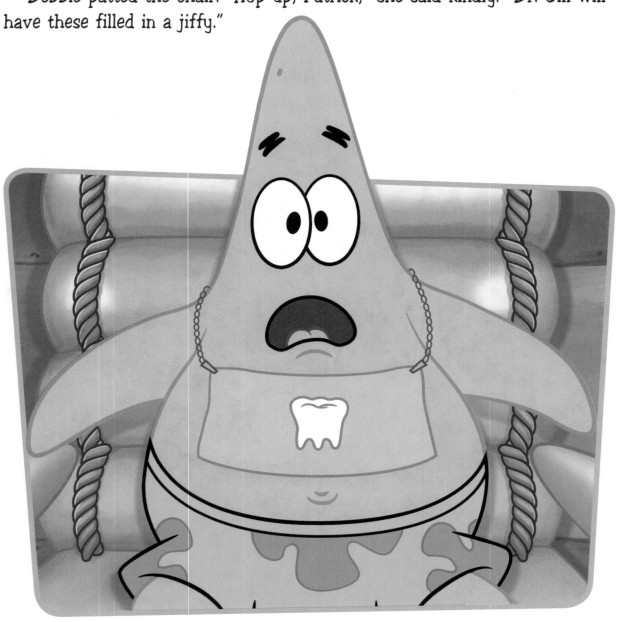

"It didn't hurt a bit!" Patrick said when Dr. Gill had finished.

"Now remember, Patrick," said Dr. Gill. "Floss your teeth every night. Brush them for at least two minutes twice a day. And come back to see me every six months! Now go pick a new toothbrush from the drawer!"

"My teeth feel so clean!" Patrick said to SpongeBob. They watched the receptionist pin another tooth with SpongeBob's name on it on the No Cavi-Tree. "Next time I come I want to see *my* name up on the No Cavi-Tree!" said Patrick.

"I'm sure you will, Patrick," said SpongeBob.